Pigs' Tales

The Amazing Journey to Apricot Farm

Gillian & Ryan Butler
illustrations by: Cilla Hocking

lllllll

First Edition Published in Great Britain 2024
Visit our website: piggytales.co.uk

Text copyright © Gillian Butler & Ryan Butler 2024
Illustrations copyright © Cilla Hocking 2024 – cillahocking.com

ISBN: 978-1-3999-8804-9

Acknowledgments

Graphic Designer: Wes Butler   Proof Reader: Caroline Towndrow
Editor: Kate Ryan   Advisor: Scott Butler

Printed and bound in England by
Acanthus Press Limited

2516052
Carbon Captured Material

For Alan

llllllll

Contents

1.

ℓℓ ℓℓℓℓℓ

Piggy-no-tail

Sometime, not too long ago, in a place not too far away, there was a piglet called Peewee.

Peewee was very young, so he was very small indeed – tiny even. But, apart from his size, there's something you should know about Peewee.

Peewee wasn't like the other piglets on Turnip Farm, because he didn't have a curly-whirly piggy tail. The other pigs on the farm found this strange. They made fun of Peewee because he didn't have a tail.

There was one pig in particular, a pig called Grunter, who was really quite nasty to Peewee. He'd say things like, "You're not a real pig, you're a pink toad! You come from a farm of animals with missing parts." When nobody else was around, he'd often grunt to Peewee, "You don't belong here."

It was Grandad Percy's birthday and celebrations were about to begin. Grandad Percy was the oldest pig on Turnip Farm, it being his 101st birthday. Seeing that everyone was enjoying the wonder- ful party

and having so much fun, Grandad decided to make a speech. "Thank you, all, for being here," he said. "I have had a wonderful life with a very special family, and I have many tales to tell."

But at that moment, nasty Grunter interrupted the speech, "Perhaps you should give one of those tails to Peewee!"

Some of the animals found this funny and started to laugh. They pointed their trotters at Peewee,

shouting "Piggy-no-tail! Piggy-no-tail!" Poor Peewee was so embarrassed and upset that he decided to run.

He ran as fast as his tiny legs could carry him until he came to the edge of the farm. There, he squeezed through a narrow hole in the fence and into a large open field. He kept running until his trotters grew tired and he couldn't go any further. Sitting down, exhausted, he began to cry. Peewee looked back at where his tail should be and wished with all his heart that his little pink body didn't end where it did. If only he had a tail!

Peewee stayed there for a long time. Where could he go? What would he do? What good is a pig without a tail?

Peewee thought about his tail. He wondered what could have happened to it. Slowly, despite his despair, Peewee began to feel a small glimmer of hope. If he'd lost his tail, it must still be out there somewhere – maybe he could find it! Peewee now knew exactly what he was going to do – he was going to search for his missing tail!

Suddenly, screeching and squalling filled the air. A flock of fierce crows swooped down from the sky and started pecking him with their evil beaks! Peewee was so scared he forgot how tired he was and ran for his life. He didn't know where he was going – he was squealing in fear – but he knew he needed to get away from the nasty birds.

Peewee ran and ran, further away from home. Eventually, the crows gave up the chase and flew off. Peewee collapsed on the ground again, exhausted. He had never been this far away from home before. Where was he? What was going to happen to him?

2.

The Kindness of a White Horse

Peewee thought about his family. He wondered if anyone was missing him, but he found it hard to believe they were. Who would miss a piglet with no tail? "This is for the best," Peewee said to himself. "I will find a place where I belong."

The sky above him was beginning to get dark, and the clouds had turned grey and thick. A raindrop hit Peewee's snout and he looked around for shelter – it would soon be night, and he had never slept on his own before. Then, Peewee felt the ground under his trotters begin

to shake. He could hear a noise like distant thunder; quiet at first but growing louder and louder – it sounded like it was getting nearer.

It wasn't thunder. Peewee realised he had heard a sound like this before.

It was the sound of a big horse galloping. Peewee looked up, trying to see where the horse was, but his teeny piglet eyes couldn't focus because he was so tired, and the rain-drops were getting in them. Peewee was fright-ened – the noise was very loud now and he still couldn't see anything – so he scurried to a nearby rock to hide. The galloping was very close now, almost too loud to bear. Then, all of a sudden, it stopped. Peewee tried to be as still as possible.

"Are you lost, little pig?" a deep, gentle voice asked. The big horse must have seen him.

Peewee was so scared that, for a few minutes, he didn't move a muscle. Eventually, he plucked up the courage to peep over the rock. There, he saw a big, beautiful white horse looking back at him.

"Yes," Peewee said. "I'm lost, and I can't find my tail." As he spoke, he felt his eyes fill with tears.

The white horse could see the sadness in the

little piglet's eyes and, as he was kind by nature, he wanted to help. He knelt down and invited Peewee to climb onto his back. Peewee was cautious for a moment, but there was a feeling inside him that told him he could trust this horse. So, he jumped onto the rock that he had been hiding behind, and then onto the back of the great white horse.

"I'll take you to the edge of the field, where you can go through the narrow gate and follow the long and winding path. There are many small tracks on either side, but take care to stay on the long and winding path until you come to the wooden bridge that crosses the fast-flowing river. When you cross the bridge, you will find Apricot Farm. I've heard there are some other lost animals there, like you."

The white horse started galloping with Peewee holding on to him for dear life. As they arrived at an old wooden gate, the rain began to pour. The horse knelt down and Peewee jumped off, with water running down his face. "Thank you for your help," the little pig said. "I'm Peewee. It was nice to meet you."

"My name is Sovereign," said the great white horse. "I am sure you will find what you are searching for, Peewee."

Peewee stepped through the narrow wooden gate and onto the winding path, which by now was dotted with big puddles from all the heavy rain. Even though he was soaked through and his legs still ached, Peewee had a bounce in his step. Now he knew where he was going – to find Apricot Farm.

But, first thing, first; the night was drawing in, so he would need to find a safe place to sleep.

3.

Lucky Escape

Wake up! Wake up! It's not safe for you to stay here!"

Peewee had fallen asleep in the hollow of an old tree, just off the long and winding path. He opened his eyes to see a small black dog with a slightly wonky eye and a scrunched-up face staring right at him. The dog was a pug named Puzzle.

(If you have met a pug before, you'll know that they look funny and cute all at the same time, and that when they talk, they

sound a bit like they're out of breath, even if they haven't been doing very much at all.)

Peewee jumped up at once. "Why isn't it safe here?" he asked, anxiously.

"Umm ... I can't remember," Puzzle responded, breathlessly. They both looked at each other, confused.

After a pause, the dog spoke again. "I'm sorry. Sometimes it's difficult for me to remember what I was saying."

"You mean, you've lost your words?" asked Peewee, who was wide awake now.

"Yes ... I think that's what I mean ..." Puzzle replied.

"Well, I've lost my tail and I'm on my way

to Apricot Farm to find it. We could go together.
I can find my tail, and you can find your words."

Puzzle agreed. But just as they had properly introduced themselves, a huge slithery snake appeared from the undergrowth.

"Aghhhhhhhh!!!" The two tiny
animals screamed, in great terror.

Peewee had been sleeping in the old hollow
tree, which was the snake's home. This was the
thing that Puzzle had been trying to tell him.

"Ruuunnnn!!!" squealed Peewee. And
they ran. Luckily for them, the snake
had just eaten his breakfast, so he didn't
bother to chase them. Once they realised
they weren't being chased, they stopped,
both trying to get their breath back.

"If you hadn't lost your words, Puzzle, this would never have happened. We could have been swallowed up," Peewee said angrily, between gasps of breath.

Puzzle dropped his head into his paws. "I'm sorry," he sniffled.

Seeing his friend so sad, Peewee realised he had said a horrible thing. "No, I'm sorry Puzzle; it's not your fault. If anything, you saved my bacon by waking me up in the first place. I could have been the snake's breakfast if it wasn't for you!"

Hearing this cheered Puzzle up, and they both smiled. "Where are we going, again?" Puzzle asked, looking around.

"Apricot Farm," Peewee replied.

4.

The Most Amazing Ears You've Ever Seen

Peewee felt very happy now that he had found a friend. There was a warm, fuzzy feeling in his tummy, which made the way ahead seem less scary.

Peewee and Puzzle were walking merrily along the long and winding path in search of Apricot Farm, when they heard a rustling sound coming from the bushes. They both looked at each other, wondering if they should peep into the bushes, but neither of them moved. To be honest, they were both quite scared. Peewee thought it might be the slithery snake again – maybe he had followed them, hoping to have them for his dinner!

Unexpectedly, a head popped out of the bush. They were both so surprised that Peewee nearly jumped out of his skin, and Puzzle nearly jumped out of his fur.

It was a rabbit with the most amazing, ginormous ears either of them had ever seen. One ear stood up straight while the other ear flopped down, nearly touching the rabbit's paw.

"HI!" said the rabbit in a very loud voice. "MY NAME IS HOPSTER! WHAT ARE YOUR NAMES?"

"My name is Peewee," said Peewee.

"And my name is Puzzle," said Puzzle.

"Sorry? What did you say? You'll have to speak up, I'm afraid. I'M A LITTLE DEAF!" bellowed the rabbit.

"MY NAME IS PEEWEE AND THIS IS PUZZLE!" shouted Peewee.

"Oh! So pleased to meet you!" the friendly rabbit replied. "I was just about to dig a hole to make myself a burrow. I need somewhere to sleep tonight. I've been hopping all day long and I'm extremely tired."

"Are you far from home?" Peewee asked.

"Yes, but I'm not sure where I'm going. Where are you two heading?" asked Hopster.

"We're off to find Apricot Farm. I heard from a big white horse called Sovereign that there are other lost animals like us there," explained Peewee. "We're to follow this long and winding path that leads to the wooden bridge, which crosses the fast-flowing river. When we cross the bridge, we'll be sure to find Apricot Farm."

"WOW!" Hopster shouted at the top of his voice, which was very loud. "Pleeeease may I join you on your journey?" As he was such a friendly rabbit, they both agreed without hesitation.

With that decided, it was time to find something to eat for their dinner. After a while spent foraging, they tucked into a meal of wild strawberries and blackberries, with a dandelion and nettle-leaf salad on the side. Peewee and Hopster rather enjoyed it, but Puzzle wasn't that impressed. Still, it was better than nothing, he thought.

It was soon time to get some sleep.

Hopster hopped along to his burrow for the night, while Peewee and Puzzle found a not-too-prickly bush to sleep under. They both snuggled in together, feeling snug as two bugs in a rug. In no time, Puzzle was asleep and snoring away like a pig (which Peewee thought was quite funny).

Peewee lay awake for a while, thinking about the day. He was so glad to have found another friend who wanted to join him on the quest to find Apricot Farm… and on his quest to find his tail. Peewee wondered what adventures tomorrow would bring. His eyelids were getting heavy. He gave a big sigh and drifted off into a peaceful sleep.

5.

ℓℓℓℓℓℓℓℓ

Old Memories and New Friends

Peewee was woken up by the hot sun streaming onto his delicate piglet skin. He had woken up feeling happy, but why? Ah yes! He remembered! He scrambled up and turned around on himself, trying to get a good view of his little pink bottom. He was sure he'd see it there! His curly-whirly tail!

But there was nothing there. No tail at all. He must have dreamt it.

Peewee felt a little sad, but he wasn't going to let it spoil his day. He still hoped that he would find his tail at Apricot Farm.

Puzzle was still sound asleep,

curled up in a little black furry ball. He
looked so cute. "Wake up. Wake up,
Puzzle," Peewee whispered in his ear.

Puzzle stirred, looking around and rubbing his

bleary eyes with his paws. He looked confused.

"Are we going to Apple Farm today?" he asked.

"Oh, Puzzle, you're such a special friend!" said
Peewee, smiling at him. "You're nearly right,
we are going to Apricot Farm, but I'm not sure
if we'll make it all the way there today."

Puzzle wondered if he was ever going to stop
being so confused and mixing up his words.
If only he could be like everyone else. His
thoughts wandered back to his home, where
he had been called such horrible names: "Oh,
here comes the tongue-tied wonky face!"

Those words hurt him deep inside. They made
him feel so sad that nobody understood him.
They made him feel ugly and stupid. So, one
day, Puzzle had decided to leave home, to find

a place where people loved him and understood him. He was glad to have met Peewee,
who was so kind and understanding.

Peewee noticed that the pug looked
rather sad. "Cheer up, Puzzle," he said.
"We're on an amazing journey to Apricot
Farm. Come on! Let's find Hopster."

Hopster was already up and had
eaten his breakfast of fresh
green grass (the remains of
which were hanging

out of his mouth). He was also excited about Apricot Farm. He, too, had been teased at home about his funny ears and how he never seemed to hear what anyone said. "You're such a naughty rabbit," his teacher would scold. "Why do you never listen?" She didn't believe that he wanted to learn just as badly as everyone else. Nobody ever believed that he just couldn't hear.

'Still, never mind', he thought. 'I've got Peewee and Puzzle now.' He was so thankful he had met these kind friends and was looking forward to sharing this new adventure with them.

6.

A Tree With Two Beautiful Blue Eyes

They set off after breakfast, still following the long and winding path. It seemed to go on for ever and became bumpier and rockier with every step they took. After a while, their sore little legs couldn't carry them any further. It was a scorching hot day and all the walking was making them very thirsty. So, they all agreed it was time to have a well-deserved rest. They found a shady spot under an enormous leafy tree, next to a cool, clear stream. It was such a relief for the tired, thirsty trio: now they could get a refreshing drink and have a paddle to soothe their aching feet.

"Meow! Meow!"

The three friends stopped mid-paddle, startled by the sound coming from halfway up the tree. They peered up to see a cat perched on one of the tree's great wide branches.

"Hello, could you help me, please? I'm afraid to come down!" cried a beautiful cat with the most dazzling blue eyes. "I've been here for days. I was so scared that I climbed up this tree as fast as I could and now I'm stuck."

"What frightened you so much?"
Peewee shouted up at her.

"Oh, I was running away from a sly old fox!" cried the cat. And she wailed, "Meow! Meow!" trying to catch her breath with every meow.

"Please don't cry!" said Peewee. "There's no fox down here now. You can come down and join us.

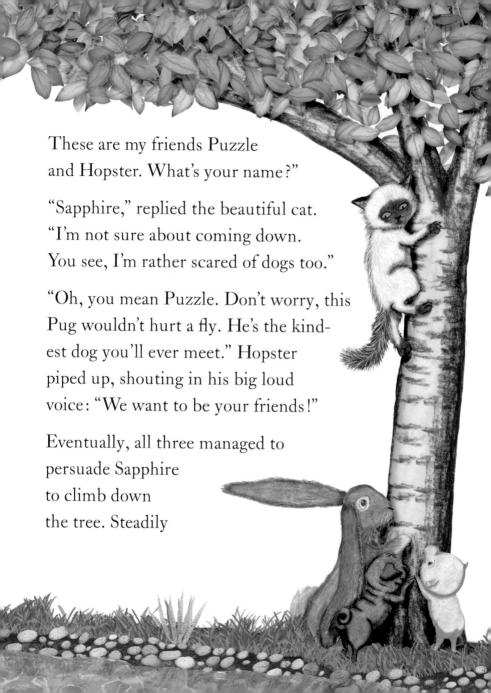

These are my friends Puzzle
and Hopster. What's your name?"

"Sapphire," replied the beautiful cat.
"I'm not sure about coming down.
You see, I'm rather scared of dogs too."

"Oh, you mean Puzzle. Don't worry, this
Pug wouldn't hurt a fly. He's the kind-
est dog you'll ever meet." Hopster
piped up, shouting in his big loud
voice: "We want to be your friends!"

Eventually, all three managed to
persuade Sapphire
to climb down
the tree. Steadily

and carefully, gripping the trunk with her sharp claws, she finally made it to the ground.

Peewee, Puzzle and Hopster all clapped. "Well done!" exclaimed Peewee.

"Why, thank you," said Sapphire. "I feel so happy to be on the ground and to have found such lovely friends. I wish I could purr to express my happiness. Normally cats purr when they're happy, but I can't purr. I don't know why."

Sapphire explained she too had left home because the other cats were so spiteful to her. Their mean voices were still going around in her mind: "Scaredy cat, scaredy cat. You're such a misery guts!" they hissed. She felt so alone because they never let her join their games. So, she had decided to leave.

Peewee told her they all knew how she felt. They all had their own bad memories and their own escape stories. He told Sapphire what Sovereign the kind horse had told him about Apricot Farm and the other lost animals. "Would you like to join Puzzle,

Hopster, and me on the journey?" he asked.

"Yes, I'd love to," she replied.

So, they continued their journey to Apricot Farm together, blissfully unaware that they were being watched. The beady eyes of the wily old fox were following them, hidden in the shadows just off the long and winding path.

7.

A Wise Leader

Up and down hills they trudged, on the long and winding path that seemed to get longer and more winding by the hour. Peewee was feeling under pressure, as he was the group's leader and they seemed to be getting nowhere fast. They reached a hilltop, from which they could see the long and winding path ahead of them, all

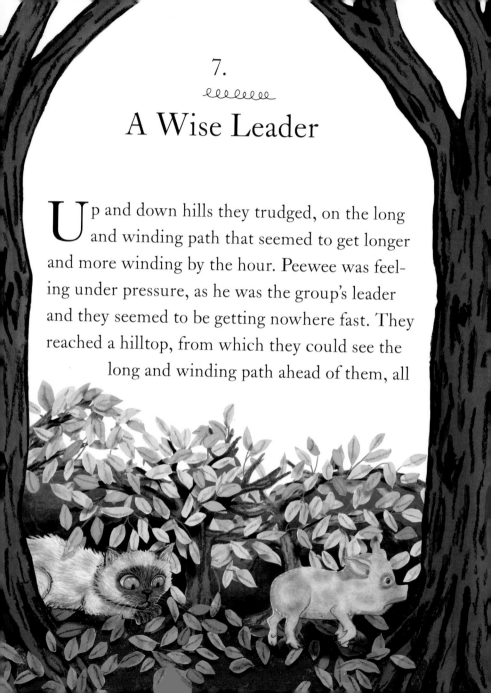

the way to the fast-flowing river in the far distance. Peewee thought he could make out the bridge, but it would take them a long time to get there.

Then he had a bright idea! If they went to the bridge in a straight line rather than down the long and winding path, they could save themselves a day of walking. They could go by cutting through the thick woods. Peewee looked at his friends and, when he saw how tired they were, he decided there and then – they'd take the shortcut. He was sure his friends would be pleased and that they probably wouldn't even notice.

He led the group into the dark woods. As they walked, the woods became thicker and thicker, and the path grew narrower. As they continued through the dark, eerie woods, they heard strange noises and owls hooting in the distance: "Too-wit

Too-woo!" Peewee was starting to get frightened, but he knew his friends were relying on him to get them through this difficult and dangerous journey.

Peewee suddenly remembered what Sovereign had said to him: "Stay on the long and winding path. Do not stray from it." He became even more worried. The dangerous journey now seemed endless and the bridge and Apricot Farm were nowhere in sight. This shortcut wasn't turning out to be so short after all – it would have been quicker to stay on the right path.

Sapphire's ears pricked up as something moved in the darkness. She had the strange feeling that the fox was still on her trail. Then a voice spoke:

"Hello little pig, what brings you through the deep dark wood? Have you lost your way?"

They all froze, terrified. Peewee was the first to come back to his senses. He saw two eyes as big as saucers looking down at them from an old oak tree. "Who are you?" he asked shakily.

"I'm Sabia, the wise old owl. We don't have too many visitors in these parts."

Peewee didn't want to admit that he had taken the wrong path. What would his friends think? But he knew that he could not continue on his journey without help. "To be honest," said Peewee, "We're trying to get to Apricot Farm. A kind white horse named Sovereign directed me to stay on the long and winding path and not to stray from it. I thought I knew better and could take a shortcut. Now I'm lost and I've led my friends astray."

Sabia replied, "It takes a wise leader to admit to making a mistake. Now you'll be able to make

your way back to the right path.
Wait until the first light of dawn,
then follow the trail that leads
in the direction of the sun.
Keep heading east, and you'll
be sure to find the long and
winding path."

The four friends decided to
take the wise old owl's advice.
They settled down to sleep
under the old oak tree and
continued their journey bright
and early the next morning.

8.

What's A Hero?

They'd been travelling for most of the day, following the wise old owl's instructions, when they reached a clearing. Hopster suddenly started yelling at the top of his voice: "There's a bridge, there's a bridge!"

"Are you sure?" asked Peewee, startled by Hopster's outburst. "We're not back on the long and winding path yet."

"Of course, I'm sure," said Hopster. "I may be hard of hearing, but I have extremely good eyesight you know. It's because I eat my carrots."

"Is that true?" Puzzle asked.

"Well, have you ever seen a rabbit wearing glasses?" retorted Hopster. Puzzle and Sapphire laughed so much their sides hurt.

In his excitement, Hopster had failed to notice that the bridge he'd seen was broken. As he made a great hop to get on to it, he suddenly disappeared down a hole between two wooden planks. Splash!

Down, down he went into the depths of the river below. Hopster couldn't swim. He tried to breathe and choked on a mouthful of water. Poor Hopster – he was disappearing under the water and he couldn't do anything to stop it.

Luckily for Hopster, one of his friends knew how to swim – in fact, they were quite an expert at the doggie paddle. Puzzle the pug came to the rescue! He jumped into the fast-flowing river, diving underneath Hopster so he could carry him on his back, safely to the riverbank. The others were so relieved that Hopster was safe.

"Meow! Meow! Are you okay, Hopster?" Sapphire cried.

Hopster was coughing and spluttering. He even had water coming out of his ears. "Yes,

thanks to Puzzle," he said. He looked at Puzzle, who was busy shaking all the water from his black furry coat. Puzzle started by shaking his head and ears and worked his way down to his back legs. He shook so much that he nearly fell back into the river.

"If it wasn't for you, I would have drowned. You're my hero," said Hopster.

Puzzle was puzzled. "What's a hero?" he asked.

Peewee replied: "Someone who is very brave and strong, just like you."

"Wow! I'm a hero, I'm a hero, I'm a hero!" He kept repeating the words and wagging his tail at the same time.

Hopster came over to him, putting his paws around his friend's podgy wrinkly head and giving him a big hug. "Puzzle, you saved my life." For perhaps the first time, Puzzle started to feel the warm glow of feeling good about himself.

Sapphire had stopped crying by this point, and soon the four friends laid down together, in one big, exhausted huddle. They'd had enough for one day. They were fast asleep before the moon appeared in the star-dotted sky.

What a day! What would tomorrow bring? What about the broken rickety-rackety bridge? How were they ever going to get across the fast-flowing river to reach Apricot Farm?

9.

Brand New Day

The four animals woke up one by one, yawning and stretching after a long, deep sleep. They stared at the river, which had turned a sparkling gold colour in the light of the rising sun. They all knew that this fierce, fast-flowing river was the only thing separating them from their destination. All they had to do was to reach the other side.

"It's a brand-new day," said Peewee, breaking the silence. "And I've got a good feeling about this one."

The three others nodded their heads in agreement.

Then one of them cried, in his very loud voice:
"I can see it now! I knew it!"

"What Hopster? What can you see?" demanded
a wide-eyed Puzzle.

"I wasn't sure last night, but now, in daylight,
I'm certain." Hopster had an expres-
sion of great satisfaction on his face.

"What are you so certain of?"
asked Sapphire. Hopster now
had everyone's full atten-
tion. The suspense
was too much for
Puzzle: "Please! Tell
us what you can see!"

"I can see another bridge. We just
need to follow the riverbank and
we'll be there in no time."

But Peewee intervened: "We're not going to take another shortcut. We are going to rejoin the long and winding path –it will take us to the bridge."

The others could barely see what Hopster was talking about, but they trusted their friend's extraordinary vision. All the animals were very excited by this news and kept jumping up and down and hugging each other. (Puzzle had forgotten why they were all so happy, but he was enjoying the jumping and hugging, so he carried on anyway.)

Once they'd calmed down a bit, the friends set off, and it didn't take them much time to reach the long and winding path. From there, they could see the path along the riverbank more clearly, and it was full of potholes and broken branches. Peewee knew he had made the right decision not to take the shortcut. The closer they got to the bridge, the more convinced they were that it was stronger and safer than the one they had tried to cross the previous day. Surely this would be the bridge that would take them to Apricot Farm!

All of the friends had a new spring in their step, apart from Hopster who had a new spring in his hop. They stepped onto the new bridge confidently and before they knew it, they were three-quarters of the way over and heading at a good pace towards the bank opposite.

Then, all of a sudden, they were stopped in their tracks.

10.

Battle on the Bridge

The four friends all jumped back in surprise. They were face to face with a beady-eyed fox.

Sapphire recognised him straight away. He was the sly old fox who had chased her up the tree, and she was sure that he had followed them through the woods. Her fur stood up on end and she quivered and shivered all over with fear. She was sure he recognised her too, but he pretended not to.

"Well, hello," he said, in a charming voice. "My name is Felon. And where are you little ones off to? Are you lost?"

It was Peewee who answered. "We're not lost. We are on our way to Apricot Farm." He pointed his little trotter towards some buildings further down the path, along the river.

"Oh, my dears. I'm afraid you have made a mistake. That's not Apricot Farm. I'm sorry to have to be the one to tell you this, but Apricot Farm was burnt down years ago. I'm sorry that you've travelled all this way for nothing."

Peewee couldn't believe it. Why had Sovereign lied to him? He had led his friends on a wild goose chase. He wanted to cry, but he managed to stop himself.

Puzzle could see the disappointment in Peewee's face. "Never mind, Peewee. We still have each other."

Hopster agreed: "Yes, Peewee, without you we'd never have found out what we're capable of. You've guided us on a great adventure and from now on, we'll always be behind you, like a curly-whirly tail."

All the while, Felon the fox was listening to their conversation. He was a cunning fox. He had a plan – and he was up to no good. He spoke in his silky-smooth voice: "As there is no Apricot Farm, I guess you have nowhere to stay tonight. I have a warm cosy den with plenty of food and drink, which I would love to share with you. To be quite honest, I get rather lonely in that big cosy den on my own. I'd be delighted to have some company."

Felon the fox grinned from ear to ear. Little did they know he was tricking them. He wasn't planning to feed his guests but to feed himself! He

wanted to eat the four friends for breakfast, lunch and dinner!

Thank goodness Sapphire wasn't fooled. "Hissssss!" She arched her back, and all her fur stood up on its end, all the way from her head to her long bushy tail. She glared at the fox with her piercing blue eyes. "I don't believe you. You're nothing but a liar."

The fox had not planned for this. He thought the animals were stupid enough to believe his nasty schemes. He knew he had to act quickly.

"You have no trees to hide in this time, Kitty" he snarled. He sprung towards Sapphire, expecting her to run away, but she pounced on to his face and stuck her long claws into his nose.

The fox cried out in pain and tried to shake her off. Sapphire tightened her grip on his face and bit a piece out of his ear. The frenzied fox screamed in pain and tried to shake her off again. Sapphire jumped up onto the narrow wooden railings, hissing down at the fox.

Felon wasn't going to let his dinner attack him and get away with it! The frustrated fox leapt onto the thin wooden railing, ready to continue the fight, but his paws were much bigger than Sapphire's

and the rail was very narrow. Felon lost his grip
and fell off the bridge. The four friends watched
with open mouths as the nasty fox fell, fell, fell,
and landed in the water below. In an instant,
he was swept away by the fast-flowing river.

It was Hopster who recovered his wits first. "Well, I imagine that's the last time he'll be calling you a scaredy cat!" he boomed.

The four friends laughed in relief and amazement at how brave Sapphire had been.

11.

A Place To Belong

The friends stayed close to each other as they walked down a path bordered by beautiful apricot trees.

Finally, they came to a wooden gate engraved with the words 'APRICOT FARM'. They had arrived.

Peewee gazed at his new-found friends and was so grateful to have them there by his side. Leaving home seemed like a lifetime ago. Each of them had discovered hidden strengths during their adventure together: Peewee had discovered that he was a great leader; Puzzle had found the hero inside him; Hopster's sharp eyes had helped

them find their way, and he'd cheered them up in times of despair; and Sapphire had found courage from deep within to see off the sly fox.

Peewee shuddered to think what might have happened to them without her. Suddenly, Sapphire began to purr.

They all pushed open the gate together and at last set foot on Apricot Farm.

As he felt his little trotter touch the wooden gate, Peewee thought about how his journey to Apricot Farm

began, and Sovereign the kind horse who had shown him which path to follow. As he thought about the beautiful white horse, it was as though Peewee could even hear his galloping hooves getting louder and louder. It seemed so real.

"Hello, Peewee," said a loud clear voice. The piglet shook his head in disbelief – but he wasn't daydreaming. There, in front of him, was the great white horse.

"Welcome to Apricot Farm," said Sovereign.

Peewee was confused. Why was Sovereign at the farm? Had he travelled here too? Peewee started to feel a little bit angry: Sovereign had seen that Peewee was lost and alone. He could have taken him all the way to Apricot Farm on his back! Why didn't he?

Peewee was getting angrier and angrier until he couldn't hold it in any longer. "Why did you leave me?" he squealed at Sovereign.

Sovereign smiled. "You're quite right, Peewee," he said in his deep gentle voice. "I could have carried you on my back and made it easy for you, but if I had, who would you be now?"

Peewee looked up at Sovereign and thought hard. "I would be the same scared and sad piglet I was when I hopped on your back and I would never have met my amazing friends, Puzzle, Hopster and Sapphire," he said, slowly.

"Indeed, you are right. The moment your feet hit the ground, your journey of self-discovery began. Peewee, you faced many obstacles and trials on your journey, but you were able to overcome them. I knew that you would make it." Still smiling,

Sovereign lowered his long neck and kissed the four friends, whispering soft, encouraging words in each of their ears. The friends felt so loved and accepted which filled them with great joy.

Sovereign invited them to live on Apricot
Farm, where they met many more animals who
had found a place to belong, just like them.
Peewee went on to have many more adventures, much bigger adventures than a little pig
could ever dream of. And in every one of them,
his friends were by his side. The little piglet
was so happy, he forgot he'd been looking for
his tail. In fact, he forgot to miss his tail at all.

The End...